Childhood Is a Time of Innocence

Twentieth Anniversary Edition

JOAN WALSH ANGLUND

Childhood

Is

a

Time

of

Innocence

Harcourt Brace & Company

San Diego   New York   London

By Joan Walsh Anglund

A FRIEND IS SOMEONE WHO
   LIKES YOU
THE BRAVE COWBOY
LOVE IS A SPECIAL WAY OF
   FEELING
IN A PUMPKIN SHELL
COWBOY AND HIS FRIEND
CHRISTMAS IS A TIME OF GIVING
NIBBLE NIBBLE MOUSEKIN
SPRING IS A NEW BEGINNING

COWBOY'S SECRET LIFE
CHILDHOOD IS A TIME OF
   INNOCENCE
WHAT COLOR IS LOVE?
MORNING IS A LITTLE CHILD
DO YOU LOVE SOMEONE?
A GIFT OF LOVE
CHRISTMAS IS LOVE
LOVE IS A BABY
PEACE IS A CIRCLE OF LOVE

For adults
A CUP OF SUN

Library of Congress Cataloging-in-Publication Data
Anglund, Joan Walsh.
Childhood is a time of innocence/Joan Walsh Anglund.
p. cm.
Summary: Describes the essence of childhood in brief text and illustrations.
ISBN 0-15-216952-0
I. Title.
PZ7.A586Ch   1991
[E]—dc20   91-15832

Printed in the United States of America

L M N O

for patsy
who was with me

Childhood is a time of innocence.

It is the morning time of life
when all is change and wonder.

It begins with being born
and ends with growing up.

It is a small world of pennies and wishes . . .

of sudden friendships . . .

and short sorrows.

It is big stairs and small footprints.

It is joy . . . and laughter . . .
and make-believe.

Childhood is a magic place of dreams . . .
where everything is possible
and the best is just beginning.

It is a timeless place . . .
   where minutes are not numbered
      and the hours are sweet with happiness.

Childhood is for exploring. . . .

It is for running . . . and reaching . . .
and touching . . . and seeing . . .
and tasting . . . and hearing . . .
and learning . . .

but, mostly, it is for growing.

Childhood is when we are young.

It is the happy hour . . .
    the passing dream . . .
        the tender time of innocence
that is part of us forever.